To Justin, Kim, Ruth, and Will, who make Christmases merry and magical - *P. T.*

For Jenna - *J.*

 First U.S. edition 2017. Library of Congress Catalog Card Number 2017953747. ISBN 978-0-7636-9571-2.
This book was typeset in OPTIMemphis. The illustrations were done in pencil, chalk, and paint and colored digitally.
Candlewick Press, 99 Dover Street, Somerville, Massachusetts 02144. visit us at www.candlewick.com.
Printed in Heshan, Guangdong, China. 19 20 21 22 LEO 10 9 8 7 6

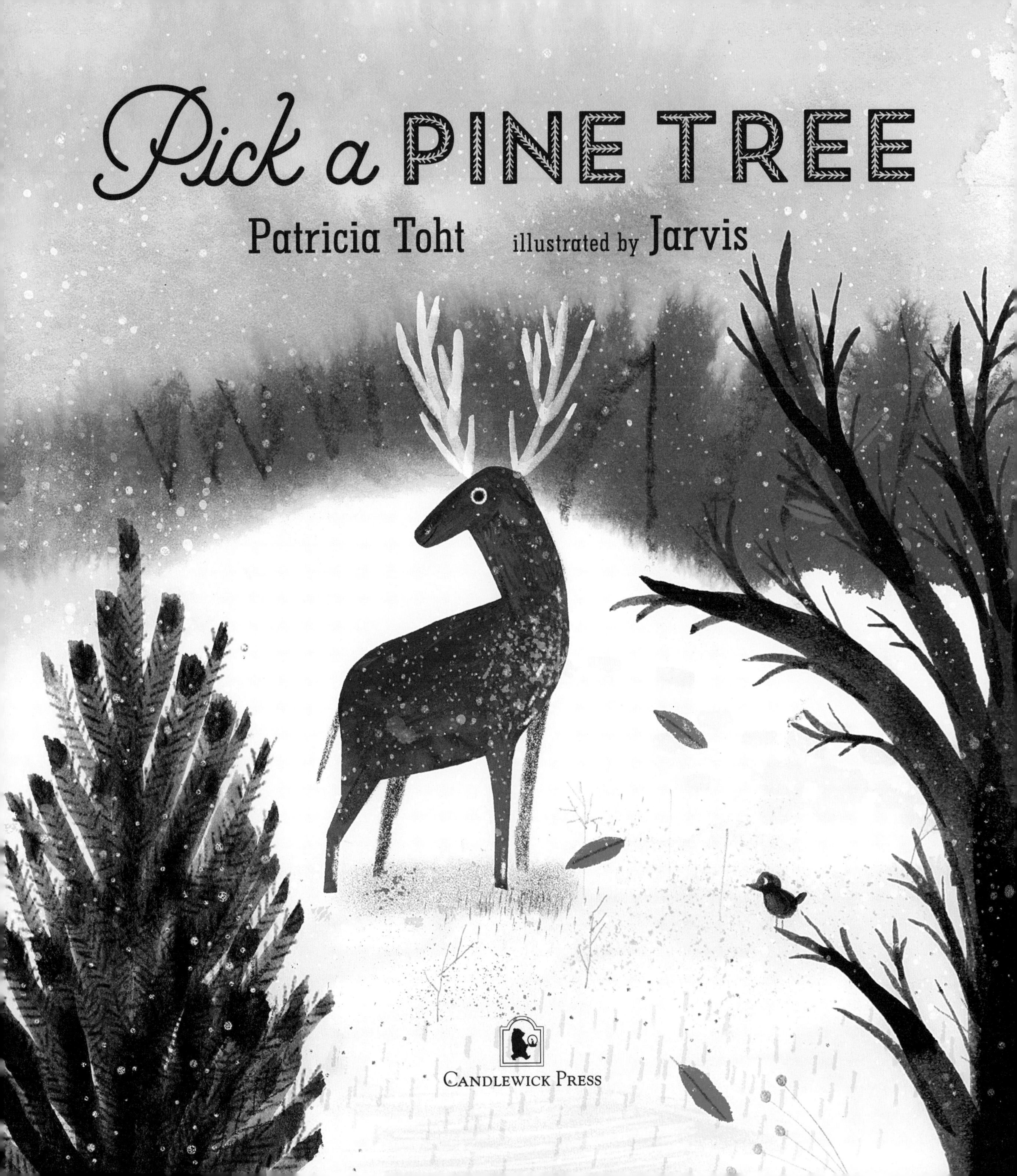

Pick a PINE TREE

Patricia Toht illustrated by Jarvis

CANDLEWICK PRESS

Pick a pine tree
from the lot—

PINE
TREES
FOR
SALE

slim and tall
or short and squat.
One with spiky needle clumps,
scaly bark, or sappy bumps.

Long, straight limbs
or branches bent—
mmm! Just smell
that piney scent!

Lift the tree
above your head;
bundle it upon your sled,

or, if you live very far,
bring it home
atop your car.

Now . . .

move aside a lamp or chair;
clear away a section where
your tree will sit, tall and grand,
snug and sturdy, in its stand.

Trim the trunk
a little bit,
just enough
so it will fit.

Slip it in and
turn screws tight—
they will hold
your tree upright.

Fill with water
to the brink.
Give your thirsty
tree a drink!
Then . . .

find the trimmings
stored within
bulging boxes, rusty tins,
paper bags, a wooden case.

Bring them to that
special place,
there, beside your tree.

But wait . . .

don't decorate alone!
Call some people
on the phone.

Ask your friends
to come and stay—

host a
decorating
day!

Stretch along some
twinkling lights,
a colored mix
or simply white.
Fat, round bulbs
or pointy tips,
bubble lights or
candle clips.

Start up top
or near the base;
wrap around
and tuck in place.
Next . . .

hang ornaments
upon your tree.
What kind of trinkets
will they be?

Jolly Santas.
Dancing elves.
Wooden reindeer.
Jingle bells.
Lacy snowflakes.
Paper dolls.

Candy canes and
bright glass balls.
With loops of thread
or wire hooks,
hang them all in
little nooks.

Add the final
touches now—
garlands strung
from bough to bough.

Strands of tinsel
on the tips,
falling down
in silver drips.
Then . . .

grab a footstool.
Climb right up.
Set something
wonderful on top.

A golden star.
A velvet bow.
An angel dressed
in flowing robes.

Lay a tree skirt
down below.
Add some houses
flecked with snow,

a train that chugs
around a track,
secret presents
in a sack.

At last, it's time
to make it SHINE!
Plug in lights
along the floor.

LOOK!

It's not a pine tree anymore.

It's a . . .

CHRISTMAS
TREE!

Gather round the tree to sing; let your joyful voices ring.

Celebrate as nighttime falls . . .

SEQUENCING STORIES

Building a Snowman

MEG GAERTNER

Published by The Child's World®
1980 Lookout Drive • Mankato, MN 56003-1705
800-599-READ • www.childsworld.com

Photographs ©: MN Studio/Shutterstock
Images, cover (left), cover (middle left),
cover (middle right), cover (right), 3 (left), 3
(right), 5, 6, 9, 10, 13, 14, 17, 18, 21

ISBN 9781503835061
LCCN 2018963102

Printed in the United States of America
PA02425

About the Author

Meg Gaertner is a children's book author and editor. She lives in Minnesota, where there is plenty of snow each winter for making snowmen. When not writing, she enjoys dancing and spending time outdoors.

CONTENTS

Snow Time!

Ellie puts on her winter coat and mittens. She pulls on her hat. She runs outside. It snowed yesterday. That means it is time to build a **snowman**! Ellie starts by making a **snowball**.

Ellie wears a coat, hat, and mittens to stay warm and dry in the snow.

The sisters work together to push the big snowball.

At first, Ellie's sister just watches. But now she wants to help, too! Ellie and her sister push the snowball. The snowball picks up more snow. It gets bigger. After a while, they have a huge ball of snow. This will be the snowman's **base**.

Once the base is done, Ellie and her sister begin making the snowman's middle. Many snowmen have three parts. The middle goes on top of the base.

You can also make a
snow woman, a snow kid,
or even a snow animal.

You need wet snow
that packs together well
to build a snowman.

Snow is heavy. It is hard to lift the snowball. Ellie and her sister need help. Just then, their dad joins them outside!

As soon as it is ready, Ellie's dad lifts the big snowball. He puts it on top of the snowman's base. Ellie and her sister help.

Fun Fact

The tallest snowman ever was as tall as 20 adults standing on top of each other!

Do not be afraid to ask an adult for help if you need it.

The sisters work carefully so they do not knock over the snowman.

Next, Ellie and her sister add snow to the snowman. They want each part to be round like a ball. They want the snowman to look good!

Finally, it is time to make the snowman's head. Ellie makes a snowball while her sister watches. It is smaller than the snowman's base and middle.

Playing in the snow with friends and family is a lot of fun.

Do not try to lift things that are too heavy for you.

When the head is done, Ellie lifts it. She can carry it by herself. She brings it to the rest of the snowman.

Fun Fact

More than 12,000 snowmen were built during a festival in Japan. There were more snowmen than people!

At last, the snowman is done! For the final touch, Ellie adds thin branches for arms. Her sister brings leaves for the snowman's eyes and mouth.

Ellie and her sister hug their new snowy friend.

Fun Fact

Many snowmen have a carrot for a nose.

What else could Ellie
add to her snowman?

Glossary

base (BAYSS) The base is the lowest part of something. Many snowmen have a base, a middle, and a head.

festival (FESS-tuh-vuhl) A festival is a celebration that is often held at the same time each year. Many people made snowmen during a Japanese festival.

snowball (SNOH-bawl) A snowball is a ball of snow that has been tightly packed together. The head of a snowman is a snowball.

snowman (SNOH-man) A snowman is a set of large snowballs made to look like a person. Ellie and her sister built a snowman.

To Learn More

BOOKS

Fretland VanVoorst, Jenny. *Snow*. Minneapolis, MN: Bullfrog Books, 2017.

Gleisner, Jenna Lee. *A Fun Winter Day*. Mankato, MN: The Child's World, 2018.

Rice, Dona. *Studying Snowflakes*. Huntington Beach, CA: Teacher Created Materials, 2019.

WEBSITES

Visit our website for links about building a snowman:

childsworld.com/links

Note to Parents, Teachers, and Librarians: We routinely verify our Web links to make sure they are safe and active sites. So encourage your readers to check them out!

Index

The author wishes to thank Phyllis, Joanna, Marilyn, Laura,
her family, and always, Chris

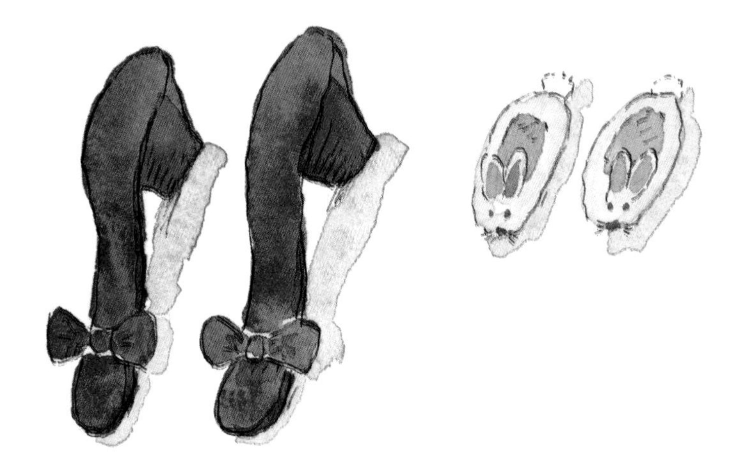

When I Was Little
A Four-Year-Old's Memoir of Her Youth

Library of Congress Cataloging-in-Publication Data
Curtis, Jamie Lee, date
When I was little: a four-year-old's memoir of her youth / by Jamie Lee Curtis; illustrated by Laura Cornell.
p. cm.
Summary: A four-year-old describes how she has changed since she was a baby.
ISBN 0-06-021078-8. — ISBN 0-06-021079-6 (lib bdg.)
ISBN 0-06-443423-0 (pbk.)
[1. Babies—Fiction. 2. Growth—Fiction.] I. Cornell, Laura, Ill. II. Title.
PZ7.C948Wh 1993 91-46188
[E]—dc20 CIP
AC

For Annie
~J.L.C.

For Lilly
~L.C.

TV

When I was little, I was a baby.

When I was little, I cried a lot.
Now I use words.

No

When I was little, I didn't know I was a girl.
My mom told me.

When I was little, I had *silly* hair. Now I can wear it in a ponytail or braids or pigtails or a pom-pom.

When I was little, I didn't get to eat Captain Crunch or paint my toenails bubble-gum pink.

When I was little, I spilled a lot.
My mom said I was a handful.
Now I'm helpful.

When I was little, I rode in a baby car seat. Now I ride like a grown-up and wave at policemen.

When I was little, I went to Mommy and Me.

Now I go to nursery school and I have teachers and cubbies and naptime and secrets.

YELL
REEN
RED

When I was little, I didn't understand time-outs.
Now I do, but I don't like them.

CAP'N CRUNCH
scoopeeloo

When I was little, I made up words like
"scoopeeloo."
Now I make up songs.

When I was little, I swam in the pool with boys. I still do, but now we wear bathing suits but we don't wear floaties.

When I was little, the slide at the park was so big.

Now it's smaller, but I still like my granny to wait at the bottom for me.

When I was little, I ate goo and yucky stuff.

Now I eat pizza and *noodles* and fruit and Chee-*tos*.

When I was little, I had two teeth.
Now I have lots, and I know how to brush them.

When I was little, I slept in a zoo.
Now I sleep in a big bed and get to play monkey.
Night Cream

When I was little, I kissed my mom and dad good night every night.
I still do, but only after they each read me a book and we play tickle torture.

When I was little, I didn't know what a family was.
When I was little, I didn't know what dreams were.
When I was little, I didn't know who I was.

Now I do!